MAGIC

Gemini

# Egyptian Adventure

Written by Kate Cary
Illustrated by Derick Bown

# HENDERSON
PUBLISHING LTD

©1997 HENDERSON PUBLISHING LTD

# Contents

# 1. Edfu: City of the Lost Pharaoh

Gemma sat on the floor in her bedroom, poring over a book full of pictures of pyramids, pharaohs and Egyptian queens.

"Magda and I are taking a short trip to Egypt next month," Mum had announced casually at the beginning of the holidays. "You know Magda – we'll probably spend our time touring the bazaars so that she can spend vast amounts of money on exotic souvenirs! How would you like to come?"

Gemma had stared in wonder. Egypt! Just herself, Mum and Mum's mad friend, Magda.

"Wow! Yes please!" she had replied. She could hardly believe it!

With delight, Gemma had raided her dad's study and the big bookcase in the living room for anything she could find out about Egypt. She had hogged the computer for a whole evening, scouring the Internet for information.

Now it was the night before the journey. Her bags were stuffed with clothes and her head was crammed with pictures and facts, ready for the morning flight to another world.

On the floor in front of her, she admired a full-page picture of Cleopatra. The Egyptian queen's black hair was bobbed in the style of the Sphinx. She wore a pleated white robe, and was decked out in jewellery made from every possible precious metal and priceless stone.

Staring at Cleopatra's finery, Gemma suddenly noticed the queen's necklace. Its green beads and purple patterned stones reminded her of another necklace. She had also seen black pearls like that before. Unfolding her legs, Gemma rummaged underneath her bed to find her jewellery box. Lifting the lid, she began to scrabble through the tangle of baubles and bracelets until she found what she was looking for. She lifted a necklace out of the box. Dark stones, finely etched with lilac and aquamarine decoration, were strung together with smoky-black gems in a long, heavy rope of beads.

Gemma carried the necklace over to the book and laid it on the page beside Cleopatra's portrait. The likeness between the string of jewels in the picture and this one was amazing. She picked up her necklace and ran her fingers over the cold, hard beads. This was one of the necklaces she had found washed up on the beach in Cornwall. She remembered the day clearly when she had found the tiny treasure chest, and had carried it carefully home. Even then, she had felt that the jewellery inside held a magic she did not understand. Gemma was sure that this necklace, like the others, was special. She reached across the rug, took hold of the strap of her rucksack and dragged it across the floor towards her. She unzipped a tiny pocket at the front, pushed the necklace into the tight little hole, and fastened it up again.

Gemma looked at the clock. She had to be up before the sun tomorrow. She began to stack her books into two neat piles. Picking up a shiny red paperback that looked as if it had never been opened, she bent it into a gentle curve and drew her thumb across its side, allowing the pages to whirr past from beginning to end. As she glanced at the pages flickering past her face, the word 'Edfu' caught her eye. Edfu – that was the first Egyptian city they were to visit. Gemma stuck her finger into the fluttering pages and turned back to the beginning of the chapter; it was headed *Edfu: City of the Lost Pharaoh.*

"Morning!" said Gemma brightly, as she marched into the kitchen. It was still dark outside the window. Dad was holding a cup of strong black coffee.

"Here," said Mum, "you'd better have some cereal. It's going to be a long day." She handed Gemma a bowl and a packet of cornflakes. Gemma sat down at the table and emptied a big handful of cereal into her bowl.

"I read a story about Edfu last night," she began, reaching across the table for the milk.

"Apparently, right at the end of the Egyptian empire, after thousands of years of pyramids and pharaohs and secret burial chambers, just as the Romans were taking over the place..."

"Did you learn the whole history of Ancient Egypt when you were meant to be sleeping?" asked Mum.

"Listen!" continued Gemma, ignoring her mother's comment. "Everyone wanted to rule Egypt because it was a really rich country. Even the Egyptian royal family spent most of their time plotting to take over the crown. They would have murdered their own grandmothers if it had meant that they could be Pharaoh and own everything. And there was one boy, called Alexander – he was the son of the Pharaoh, and he disappeared at Edfu. Apparently, he vanished from his chariot in the middle of a procession and nobody ever saw him again. The Egyptians believed that his sister Berenice used magic to make him vanish, because his disappearance would make her next in line to the throne. But I reckon she had him kidnapped

9

and murdered." Gemma paused and waited for her parents' gasps of shock and amazement. When they did not make a sound, she continued, "His body was never found. Perhaps she had him strangled and thrown into the Nile. Or perhaps he was walled up in a mummy's tomb. Perhaps he died of starvation there, alone, in the dark!"

"Eat your breakfast," said Mum.

"But isn't it fascinating? We might see the place where he disappeared. We might even see the tomb he was shut up in or the dark street corner where he was horribly murdered, and we'd never even know it."

"He probably just ran off to join the circus," suggested Dad unenthusiastically.

"Anyway," continued Mum, "we're going to Egypt so that Magda can shop for silks, rugs and trinkets and things – not to search for dead pharaohs or to solve ancient mysteries."

"I don't know why I bother having an imagination at all," said Gemma glumly, "it's not appreciated." She spooned a tiny mountain of cornflakes into her mouth.

"How much?" asked Gemma. She was standing in front of a rickety stall in the middle of an Egyptian bazaar. She had arrived in Edfu with her mother and Magda last night, bad-tempered after a tiring journey, and had woken up refreshed to a hot Egyptian morning.

Gemma pointed to a small golden statuette of a cat, encrusted with tiny fragments of green coloured glass. The stallholder smiled broadly and held up six fingers.

Gemma had been in the bazaar for an hour now and she was getting used to the Egyptian style of shopping. Magda had warned her to haggle over every price. Gemma held up three fingers. The stallholder waved four fingers back at her and gave a stern frown.

"Three," said Gemma firmly, standing her ground. The stallholder frowned for a moment longer and then his face collapsed back into a grin. He clapped his hands with joy as Gemma reached into her rucksack for her money. She

11

rummaged through old sweet wrappers and empty biros, pushing her pocket torch out of the way. As she grasped her purse, she felt the smooth, cool beads of the Cleopatra necklace rub against her fingers. She pulled out her purse and paid for the statuette.

Still glowing from her little triumph, Gemma looked around the bazaar. The stalls were packed closely together, and the small gaps between buzzed with people. She could just see her mum and Magda amidst the crowd. They were hunting through bundles of silks while a bright-eyed Egyptian merchant chattered and smiled and waved his hands at them.

Behind the bazaar, Gemma could see the solid Temple of Horus, outlined against the blue sky. It towered over the city. All the guidebooks had mentioned it; it had been built around two thousand years ago, in honour of the falcon-headed god, Horus. Its massive walls were decorated with gigantic carvings, and even now, among the more modern city buildings, it looked imposing.

Gemma preferred the smaller, more cluttered world of the bazaar. The stalls around her were swamped with colourful goods. There was everything she could imagine: mountains of fabrics, piles of spices, carpets, watches, radios, tasty-looking pies, red lumps of raw meat, and crates overflowing with rainbow-coloured vegetables. Gemma could smell the goods, mingled with the exotic aroma of Egyptian herbs and the earthy odour of dung. It made the well-ordered supermarkets back home seem bare and antiseptic.

Now seemed the perfect time to slip away. Ever since she had squeezed the necklace into her rucksack, Gemma had dreamed that it would bring her adventure while she was in Egypt.

Behind the market stalls she could see a row of dingy houses. She peered between the swaying rows of rugs dangling above her head, and saw what looked like a tiny alleyway. She began to push her way towards the shadowy gap, clinging tightly to her small rucksack as she squeezed through the crowds.

A stall was leaning precariously against one of the houses. It was stacked with clocks, watches and transistor radios.

Gemma dodged past it, and ducked into the alley.

It was empty, just as she had hoped. The noise of the bazaar was muffled here. Leaning against the rough, sandy side of a house in the cool of the shadows, she reached into her bag and slowly drew out the necklace. Butterflies began to buffet the inside of her stomach. This is no time for nerves, thought Gemma. After all, this necklace couldn't possibly take me any-where more strange or unfamiliar than this place. She glanced around to make sure that no one was watching. Then she lifted the necklace to her throat, reached around behind, and fastened the string of beads at the back. The beads felt cool around her hot neck. She could hear a voice in her head, chanting,

*You shall journey far and wide*
*Across Time's endless seas...*

And as the voice chanted, Gemma felt herself falling down, down, down, down...

## 2. Runaways

Gemma staggered slightly as the world came to an abrupt halt. She reached out her hand to steady herself and felt the gritty texture of a sandy wall beneath her fingertips. That's odd, she thought. She had expected the world around her to have changed, but the wall felt no different; it felt exactly like the wall she had leaned against before she put the necklace on. She spun around. The alleyway appeared to be unchanged.

Gingerly, she crept to the entrance of the alleyway and peeped out. The hubbub of chattering voices filled her ears once more, and the bazaar bustled in front of her; everything seemed exactly the same. Gemma's heart sank. This was not a magic necklace after all. She fingered the beads, already warm from her skin, and prepared to take them off.

Then she noticed a stall leaning beside the entrance to the alleyway. It stood in exactly the same place as the stall she had passed on her way in, but the clocks, watches and radios that had weighed it down before had vanished. In their place, lamps of every shape and size were displayed.

"Oil lamps! Oil lamps! Every style and any size!" cried the stallholder. "From every known corner of the civilised world. Modern lamps made in Luxor, antique lamps from the city of Ur! Get your lamps from Khufu's Lamp Stand! We have lamps to suit all your lighting needs!"

Gemma let go of her necklace and looked more closely into the bazaar. With a thrill of excitement, she realised that she could not see a single radio or camera anywhere. The stalls which had been laden with electric spice-grinders, alarm clocks and battery-powered fans had all disappeared. Now she saw booths, surrounded by huge earthenware jars and piled high with teetering stacks of clay bowls and pots. Every piece of crockery was decorated with bold orange and black patterns and shapes, in a style that Gemma had only seen in history books.

This must be it! she thought. I must be here, in Ancient Egypt! She silently apologised to her necklace for doubting its magical powers.

In the distance, Gemma could hear the roar of a cheering crowd, the blaring of horns and the steady thumping of drums. Suddenly, people were streaming past her, thick and fast, in the direction of the uproar. A group of babbling women, dressed in long white tunics and adorned with jewels, appeared behind her. They fluttered around her and she was jostled into the river of people.

Gemma gasped with surprise. All around her, people were smiling and talking as they hustled towards the sound of the drums. None of the jabbering Egyptians seemed to be at all perturbed by Gemma's strange appearance. Dressed in a T-shirt and jeans, she looked very different from the rest of the crowd. Other girls were dressed in long robes; their shiny black hair was bobbed and neatly knotted into tiny plaits, ornamented with delicate ivory combs and pins. Many of the young men were dressed in shendjet-kilts – those knee-length skirts seen on the men in Ancient Egyptian paintings. Everyone – men and women, young and old alike – seemed to have the same beautiful brown eyes, almond-shaped and carefully outlined with black kohl. Among these smooth, olive-skinned faces, Gemma felt very conscious of her own rosy pink and white complexion, but no one seemed to notice. Everyone was too intent on following the trumpeting noise which was growing louder by the minute.

Gemma pushed and wriggled her way to the front of the crowd. She had been aiming for what she had thought was a gap in the mass of people, but it turned out to be a wide, dusty track, lined with cheering Egyptians. Gemma stood wide-eyed, watching the procession of men, horses, carts, wagons, camels and elephants. They were parading towards the Temple of Horus, which she recognised looming in the distance.

"Look Mummy, look at the tigers!"

From behind, Gemma heard the excited

voice of a young girl perched high on a pair of shoulders. Right in front of her, fifteen big cats – lions, tigers and leopards – were straining at golden leashes. A line of wooden carts lumbered behind, each piled high with treasure. Squadrons of soldiers, clanking with weapons and perfectly uniformed, marched between the wagons and a band of musicians marched after them, playing weird and wonderful instruments.

Three swaying litters followed, like elegant four-poster beds, slung between poles and held aloft on the burnished shoulders of four squat soldiers. Each soldier wore a short red shendjet-kilt with a black and gold band stretched diagonally across his bare chest. They were armed with knives which hung from their belts in leather sheaths. Woven into the centre of each chest band Gemma could make out a symbol; it seemed vaguely familiar. She peered more closely; the golden head of a falcon lay on top of what looked like a cross made from a shepherd's crook and a bundle of wheat.

Between the posts and the curtains of
the first litter, amid a sea of silken
cushions, sat a stern-looking man. He was
beautifully dressed in white and gold. On

his head was fixed a tall, straight hat. It was striped in blue and white and encrusted with jewels.

The second litter carried a pretty young woman. A delicate curtain of silver chain mail hung from a golden crown down to her shoulders. As Gemma watched her pass, she thought that she saw the girl peer anxiously behind to a tall, thin man following on a fierce-looking stallion. Beneath a gleaming white cloak, Gemma could see that the man was wearing a blood-red tunic, edged with brilliant silver. His almond eyes were narrowed into a glittering, poisonous gaze that made her shudder. He wore no crown, but in his right hand he carried a long, black whip.

The final litter was smaller than the others. Barely visible above a pile of cushions, peeping out from behind softly billowing curtains, Gemma could see the small, oval face of a ten-year-old boy. A thick band of gold encircled his black helmet of tiny plaits. Gemma stared as he passed. Something was nagging at her memory.

Suddenly, one of the soldiers stumbled and the boy's litter tipped to one side. Out toppled the boy in an avalanche of pale satin cushions and a flurry of curtains. His crown fell from his head and rolled away into the crowd. All around, the people rushed to help him. Amid the confusion, Gemma spotted a soldier push the litter pole from his shoulder and draw a curved silver blade from its sheath. She watched disbelievingly as he strode over to the bewildered boy and lunged at him.

In an instant she was beside the boy. The terrified look on his face told her that he had seen the knife. She grabbed his hand and dragged him behind her, through the legs of the encircling crowd. She ignored the furious shout that came from behind them and kept on running.

The two children wove their way through the crowd. They were out of the thickest part of the mob and were heading towards the bazaar. The boy ran with her now. He had recovered from his shock and was hot on her heels. Gemma looked back over her shoulder and saw the soldier struggle free from the crowd. He spotted her and the boy straight away. They were easily noticed, Gemma in her outlandish jeans and T-shirt, and the boy dressed like a prince in spotless white and glittering gold. The soldier roared and charged towards them at full speed. She looked around for a place to hide. Thinking quickly, she pulled the boy down to the ground and dragged him underneath a stall.

"Hurry!" she hissed, speaking to the boy for the first time, "or he'll see us."

The two fugitives crawled forwards, pushing their way through swathes of overhanging cloth to another stall. In every direction, Gemma could see brown legs and sandalled feet – there was no way of knowing if any of them belonged to the soldier. At that moment, she felt a tugging on her sleeve.

"Look, over there," whispered the boy and pointed. Along a distant row of tunnels, through a forest of legs, she could see the opening of a narrow lane, a way out of the bazaar and hopefully an escape route from their pursuer. It seemed to be the best chance they had. "Come on," she said.

Above, staring stupidly around the bazaar and wondering what had become of his two runaways, the soldier scratched his chin. He stared through the stalls, scanning every inch for the youngsters. He failed to notice the two small figures crawl from under the booth behind him, scurry across the crowded arcade and duck back down under the stalls on the other side. By the time he had thought to look underneath, Gemma and the boy had reached the lane and slipped away into the shadows. The soldier slowly bent down and peered into the darkness beneath the stalls, but he saw nothing except pots, pans and a few scavenging mongrels moving around in the gloom.

# 3. Soter Saves the Day

The two runaways leaned back against the cool wall of a shady side street and panted. Sweat was pouring from Gemma's forehead, and the boy's face was streaked with the sooty kohl that had run from his eyes.

"Who are you?" he said eventually.

Gemma held out a limp hand and gasped, "I'm Gemma. How do you do." The boy looked curiously at Gemma's hand, then bowed. Gemma noticed a gold medallion hanging from a slender chain around his neck. It swung forward as he leaned into his bow. It was the symbol she had seen before, woven into the uniforms of the soldiers, the one which had seemed so familiar: the head of a falcon, with a shepherd's crook and a bundle of wheat poking out from behind.

"Greetings," he said formally. "I am the son of Eugertes, first-born son and heir to the throne of Egypt."

"You're Alexander!" exclaimed Gemma. Suddenly everything fell into place. The falcon's head was the symbol of his family – she had seen it in her books. It was carved on the tombs of his relatives and engraved on brooches and rings. This was the boy she had read about, the Pharaoh's son who had disappeared from Edfu all those years ago. I must have arrived on the exact day of his disappearance, thought Gemma, and now I have saved him.

"I see you have heard of me," said Alexander regally. "Now I must return to the temple and my family."

Gemma's heart sank as she remembered the whole story. Her book had said that it was Alexander's sister, Berenice, who had plotted his disappearance. In light of this, returning to his family at the Temple of Horus was the most dangerous thing Alexander could do.

"No!" she blurted. "You mustn't! You – "

Alexander eyed her suspiciously.

"Thank you for saving my life. Now I must return to my family," he repeated.

"You will be richly rewarded for your actions," he added, looking up at her a little nervously.

It suddenly occurred to Gemma that she might not have saved Alexander after all. As far as everyone was concerned, he had disappeared, just as it had said in her book. She still could not be certain that he would ever appear again, especially if he returned straight into the arms of his traitorous sister. Gemma knew that if she really was going to save him, she must stop him from returning home.

"I don't want any reward," she told him. "I just want to make sure..." She searched for the words that might win his trust, "that your royal highness is safe."

"I will be safe with my family," the boy assured her.

"You will be safer with me," insisted Gemma. The young prince looked at her strangely.

"Well..." continued Gemma, searching for a way of explaining the danger that Alexander faced, without giving away the awful truth that it was his own sister who wanted him out of the way. "You see," she began slowly, then had a thought. "It was one of your own soldiers who attacked you, wasn't it?"

"He was a member of my own body-guard," acknowledged the prince.

"Did you expect him to betray you?" asked Gemma.

"No, the penalty for such treachery is death."

"That didn't seem to stop him, though, did it? Was he the only guard involved? What about the one who first dropped your litter? How many more are involved? Can your family protect you from your own bodyguards? Is it really safe for you to return home?" She bombarded the prince with questions – as many as she could think of – until she saw the doubt creep into his face. Then she suggested an alternative. "Wouldn't it be safer for you to stick with me until we have discovered who is behind this wicked plot?"

Alexander was really doubtful now. The excitement of the chase had evaporated and here he stood, for the first time in his life, without family, advisors, guards or slaves around him. He had never ventured so far from his home before.

Gemma saw his face cloud over, and she understood how bewildered he felt – after all, she was alone in a strange city, too. The only difference was that she had chosen to come here – Alexander had not. She gave him her biggest grin. "So, what's it like to be free of all that stuff?" she asked. Alexander frowned, bewildered by Gemma's sudden change of direction.

"All what stuff?" he asked.

"All those slaves and that horrible noise and people fussing. You looked positively overwhelmed in that litter – now you're free to do as you please." Alexander looked thoughtful for a second, but Gemma was not going to give him a chance to think. "Come on, we'd better get rid of these clothes. We stand out like a couple of sore thumbs."

"How?"

"Wait here."

Gemma squeezed the boy's hand and dashed off towards a couple of beggars who were meandering down the street towards them. Alexander heard her talking to them, but he couldn't make out what they were saying. Then he saw Gemma pull a sparkling statuette out of her bag and show it to them. Before he knew what was happening, she was leading the two scruffy beggars back towards him. Alexander took a step back.

"Don't worry," said Gemma. "These kind gentlemen have agreed to sell us their clothes."

Alexander looked amazed. The two beggars were dressed in filthy, ragged tunics. Gemma saw the prince's nose wrinkle with disdain, so she carried on quickly.

"I'll bet you a camel's weight in gold that the bodyguard is still combing the streets looking for us. He'll find us for sure if we're dressed like this. We haven't got any choice, unless you fancy ending up as a kebab before tea time." Gemma laughed, as if she was joking, but she knew that she was deadly serious. So did Alexander.

"All right," he agreed. "Where shall we get changed?"

Gemma looked at the beggars.

"This way," said the shortest of the two, and beckoned them behind the striped tarpaulin of a deserted stall.

Ten minutes later, the two men popped out into the street. One of them was clutching a small, golden cat, encrusted with tiny pieces of what looked like emerald-coloured glass. The other was pointing in the direction of a shop at the far end of the street, where the smell of hot, spicy food was drifting from an open doorway.

Gemma and Alexander stepped out after the two men. She was dressed from head to foot in beggar's rags two sizes too big for her. He started to laugh and she knew exactly why. She looked down at herself and then at Alexander who was almost unrecognisable in the tattered outfit, and then she laughed too.

"You'll have to take those off," she said when the worst of their giggling fit was over. She pointed to the gold bracelets and rings which still glittered on Alexander's wrists and hands.

"And that," she added, glancing at the gold falcon dangling around his neck, "doesn't look very beggarly."

Alexander put his hand to his chest and fingered the medallion. Then he shook his head.

"What about yours?" he asked, pointing to Gemma's necklace.

"I have to wear it. If I take it off I'll have to go back. It's – it's too hard to explain," stammered Gemma.

"I understand," said Alexander solemnly, "and I cannot take this off. It is the symbol of my house. To unfasten it would be to betray my family and my people. If you must wear yours, then I must wear mine."

Gemma could see from the grave expression on his face that he meant what he said. She decided that it would be futile arguing with him; instead, she reached out and tucked the dangling lump of gold underneath his ragged tunic.

"There we go," she said. "That should do the trick. Keep it out of sight. But take the rest off, and no one will know that we're not the beggarliest beggars who ever begged."

Alexander unfastened his bracelets and tugged off his rings, tumbling them into the piece of tattered cloth that Gemma was holding out for him. She twisted the bundle of jewellery into a knot and tucked it in with their clothes which were already bursting out from the top of her rucksack.

In some ways, it was easy to hide in a bustling, ramshackle city; the streets were busy with merchants, shoppers, travellers and entertainers, and they were cluttered with stalls and boxes. In other ways, it was hard to hide in such a place – all those prying eyes and chattering tongues. Neither Alexander nor Gemma knew the city well, and by the time the sun had begun its final slide towards dusk, they both felt utterly lost in the maze of side streets. Gemma thought it was very likely that a full-scale search for Alexander had been started by now.

"This way," she said, pointing down yet another dusty street.

"I'm hungry," complained Alexander, wiping the grime from his face with his sticky hand and brushing it off on his sleeve. "If only I had some money with me, we could buy some food." It was almost tea time, and neither Alexander nor Gemma had eaten any lunch. He looked longingly at a small stall where a man lifted crisp, steaming morsels from a pan of smoking oil that sat bubbling on top of a small clay oven. Gemma thought for a moment.

"I have an idea," she said, "but only if you agree. After all, it'd be your ring we would be selling."

"My ring?" asked Alexander, looking confused. "Oh!" he smiled, catching on to her meaning. "My ring!" He nodded enthusiastically. "Of course, why didn't I think of it?" The delicious smell from the stall was wafting temptingly towards his nose, making him feel sick with hunger.

"We'll exchange one of my rings for food. Come on!" Alexander did not hesitate. He marched straight across the street to the food stall which had been tantalising his taste buds.

Gemma followed, digging the bundle of jewellery out of her rucksack. While Alexander ordered the food, she fumbled as inconspicuously as possible for the smallest ring she could find and handed it over to the stallholder. Alexander carefully lifted a large palm leaf, heaped with

36

mouthwatering food still sizzling from the pan. The stallholder held up the ring and examined it carefully. He bit it, spat on it and polished it on his grubby sleeve, and then glanced suspiciously at the two beggar children. But he could recognise a good thing when he saw it, and, without a word, he pocketed the ring and turned to serve a tall, skinny woman who hovered nearby.

Alexander and Gemma moved away, busily picking at the stack of food on the palm leaf as they went. They stopped a little way down the street, dropped to the ground and leaned against a wall so that they could tuck into their meal properly.

They were far too busy enjoying their tasty snack to notice the stocky little man, dressed in a short red shendjet-kilt, who was making slow progress down the street towards them. Slung across his bare chest was a gold and black band, and on it was woven the head of a falcon. His progress was slow because he stopped at every stall, speaking a few words to each stallholder. Occasionally he smiled and passed coins over the counter in exchange for a piece of information. Once or twice he snarled and grunted threateningly when a shopkeeper turned away and refused to help him. Eventually he worked his way along to the food stall where Alexander and Gemma had just bought their meal.

"Have you seen a pair of children this afternoon?" he asked the stallholder menacingly. The food seller grinned slyly and asked in return, "You sound peckish. Would you like to buy a delicious morsel? For the right price I think we could find something that you might enjoy."

"I'm fussy about my food," growled the man, staring straight at the food seller. The stallholder was a reckless soul, and he did not tremble as he might have, had he known the man in the red shendjet-kilt; in fact, he seemed keen to introduce himself to the stranger.

"I am Pinar. How may I help?" he said, and bowed.

The man in the red shendjet-kilt smiled coldly, and said, "I'm Tut, and I'm hungry for information."

"We cater for all tastes here," said Pinar. "What would you like to know?"

Alexander and Gemma were busy dividing their last few mouthfuls. They had a clear view of Pinar's food stall, but they didn't notice the man in the red shendjet-kilt. Nor did they see Pinar show Tut the golden ring that Gemma had exchanged for food and point in their direction. They didn't even look up as Tut thanked Pinar with a handful of coins and began to head their way. Alexander was licking the palm leaf clean, despite its bitter taste, and Gemma was wiping her fingers on her frayed tunic when she spotted the hairy legs and solid brown knees of Tut approaching them. She looked up to see him looming above them, black against the sinking, orange sun, like the pattern on an earthenware pot. Grabbing Alexander's sleeve, she sprang to her feet. She blinked the sunspots out of her eyes, and instantly recognised the black and gold band across Tut's chest.

"How did two grubby beggar kids like you lay your hands on a ring like this?" Tut snarled the words and held up the small golden object for them to see.

Alexander was the first to answer.

"Th-that's not our ring!" He blurted out the first words that came into his head. Tut leaned towards him.

"Oh, it isn't?" he sneered in a singsong voice. "And I suppose that man over there is a LIAR!" Tut spat out the last word and raised a threatening hand to the trembling Alexander.

"We found it!" yelled Gemma. Tut snapped his head around and glared at her.

"There was this rich boy," she said hurriedly, "he was all dressed up, and covered in jewellery. I never saw anyone so grand before in my life." Gemma tried her best to sound like a poor beggar child. "This ring fell out of his pocket! We just picked it up." Tut's face relaxed into a thoughtful expression.

"Where did you see this child?" he asked, a little less roughly.

Gemma sighed with relief. "It was in the bazaar, only about half an hour ago! He might still be here," she said. She quietly grasped her rucksack, which was sitting on the ground beside her, and pointed in the direction they had come from. Tut followed her finger, and Gemma and Alexander began to sidle away.

"Hold on, how old was this boy?" asked Tut, turning back to the pair and stopping them in their tracks.

"He looked about eleven, I suppose, maybe even twelve," said Alexander hopefully. Tut looked at him and drummed his fingers on his prickly chin.

"Eleven or twelve," he said thoughtfully. Alexander nodded back, and wriggled uncomfortably against the wall.

"Maybe twelve," repeated Alexander, and fidgeted some more. Unfortunately, this time Alexander had fidgeted a fidget too much, and his pendant slid through a hole in his shabby tunic. A final ray of the setting sun glinted off the golden falcon's head and sparkled right into Tut's eyes.

Tut reacted quickly, grabbing the necklace and clutching it through the tattered cloth so that the falcon dangled on to his fist. Alexander staggered behind.

"So, you saw a rich boy?" said Tut nastily. "I think *you* are a rich boy!" With his other hand, he began to rub the dirt from Alexander's face in order to get a better look at him.

"Here," shouted Gemma, "look what's in this!" She swung her rucksack up off the ground, and clouted Tut on the side of the head. He was thrown off balance and swayed slightly, letting go of Alexander as he struggled to remain upright. For the second time that day, Gemma grabbed Alexander's hand and the two children ran for all they were worth.

"Stop them!" yelled Tut, raising the alarm. At the sound of his cry, more soldiers seemed to appear from nowhere. In front of Gemma and Alexander, blocking the end of the street, three burly guards lined themselves up and stretched out their arms to trap the fleeing children.

"This way!" shouted Gemma, catching a small glimpse of guard-free space where a fruit stand leaned against a wall. The two children dived underneath it and out the other side. They turned the corner and raced away down the next street. The guards turned and sped after them.

"Down here!" cried Gemma, grabbing Alexander's sleeve and steering him at full pelt down a narrow side street.

The street was cloaked in shadow now that the sun had sunk below the city skyline, and it was growing darker and narrower with every desperate stride.

"I think we've chosen a dead end," gasped Alexander, as the buildings closed in on each side.

"This way then," suggested Gemma, pointing to an open staircase that ran up one storey to the roof of a small building.

They raced up the stairs, two at a time, and on to the sandy open roof. They tore across the rooftop and leaped down on to the roof next door. Behind, seven soldiers emerged from the staircase and stumbled after them.

All the roofs of the city seemed to spread out before them in the twilight. Gemma and Alexander leaped and dived nimbly from one to the next. Suddenly, Gemma spied a gap in the rooftops in front of them where an alleyway separated the houses.

"Jump!" she screamed to Alexander, as they hurtled towards it.

They landed with a thud on the other side. The soldiers were trailing quite a distance behind them now, but the two children were exhausted.

Gemma caught sight of a flight of stairs leading down into another dark street. The shadows should make it easier to hide. She waved her idea to Alexander and the two children ran down the dusty steps and into the street. At the bottom, Gemma looked hurriedly around for a hiding place.

Light streamed out of a doorway a few yards further on. She could make out the fat shape of a man. He was surrounded by yapping dogs, and he appeared to be feeding them scraps from a large bowl.

"Hungry, eh? Well, don't you worry. Soter has a little dinner for all of you, as usual." He paused. "Hey, do you hear something? Is that more friends I see in the shadows? Come closer, so Soter can see you."

Behind them, Gemma could hear the

guards on the roof, thundering towards the staircase. In desperation, she stepped forward, out of the shadows. Nervously, Alexander followed her.

"Aha!" said Soter. His voice seemed to smile even before his face broke into a welcoming grin. "I thought I heard two little mice in the shadows. You hungry?" He spotted the weariness on Alexander's face immediately, and he saw Gemma glancing fearfully over her shoulder. He, too, could hear the hammering footsteps of the guards overhead.

"You are in need of a quiet place to rest, perhaps?" he suggested. Gemma and Alexander nodded, too tired and frightened to worry about where they were heading, but desperate to find a place to hide.

"Come with me," said Soter gently, and he held his door wide open and beckoned the two children inside.

# 4. Neos Has a Plan

When Alexander and Gemma had finished panting, they straightened up and saw that they were standing in a large, warm kitchen.

"I am Soter, the baker." The fat, smiling man stretched his arms wide and introduced himself properly. "This is where I work."

Gemma looked around. The corners of the room were lit with oil lamps, and every wall flickered with light. One wall seemed to be given up entirely to a line of heavy oven doors. Along another wall, large sacks and barrels were neatly lined up. In the middle of the room stood a low, wide wooden table, scrubbed and empty after a busy day's baking.

"Are you hungry?" asked Soter. Gemma and Alexander shook their heads; their last meal was still churning around inside them.

"A drink perhaps?"

Gemma licked her dry lips. A drink would be very welcome. She nodded.

Soter trotted over to a large, clay jug, poured water into two wooden cups and carried them over to Gemma and Alexander. He watched as they drank, and took the cups from them when they had finished.

"Now," he said, "are you two going to tell Soter why you are being chased by those men?" Alexander looked at Gemma, and Gemma looked back at Alexander giving a tiny shake of her head. She felt that it was not safe to tell anyone who they were or why they were on the run. She spoke first.

"We can't tell you why we're running away," she said honestly, "because our lives may be in danger if we do."

"Are you thieves?" asked Soter. He looked the two shabbily dressed children up and down.

"No," replied Gemma firmly. She lifted her chin and stared Soter straight in the eye. He paused for a moment, then smiled the same warm smile he had used to greet them.

"In that case, would you like to sleep here tonight? I must return home to my family, but here it is warm and quiet, and you will be safe." Alexander and Gemma smiled with relief.

"Oh, yes please," they answered happily.

Soter poured enough oil into a lamp to last them the whole night, and took two loaves out of his basket for their supper before he left. He put another layer of logs over the embers at the bottom of his huge oven, so that it would be ready to stoke up into a fierce bread-baking fire in the morning.

"Bolt the door after I have gone. I shall be back at sunrise. Sleep well; may the god Ra be watching over you." He pulled the door shut, and Alexander and Gemma were left alone.

"Are you tired?" asked Gemma.

"A little," replied Alexander.

She wandered over to the pile of empty sacks that were heaped beside the line of barrels and dragged a handful over to the warm oven wall. A clear sky had cast a chill over the city.

"Here," she said. "Lie down and rest."

Alexander looked at the heap of hessian on the hard earth floor and tried not to think of the fine smooth sheets which stretched over his soft mattress at home.

"It'll be all right," Gemma reassured him. The sorrowful look on his face was hard to miss. "You'll be home before long, and everything will be back to normal."

Alexander gave her a brave smile and lay down on the pile of sacks. He fidgeted and shuffled, but soon lay still.

Gemma waited until he was fast asleep, and then she slipped on her sandals. She crossed the room, unbolted the latch on the door and slipped out into the alleyway.

It was very dark by now, but the sky was clear, and by the light of the half-moon Gemma could see the Temple of Horus in the distance, towering above the tiny houses of Edfu. Alexander had said his family was there, so that was the place where Gemma must go if she was to save him. She had to find out more about the plot against him. She knew who had engineered it, from her book, and it was up to her to find his treacherous sister and discover what she was up to.

There were no streetlamps to light the way, only an occasional bright stream from a lighted window and a thin blue strip of moonlight along the centre of the lane. But

Gemma welcomed the cover of darkness. She wandered from street to street, through twisting passages and along winding alleys, always keeping the temple in front of her. As she went, she made a mental note of each shuttered shop and ornate balcony, drawing a map in her mind to help her find the way back to Alexander later.

Gradually, the temple loomed larger and larger above the buildings as she advanced nearer and nearer. Then, suddenly, she emerged from a small street and saw the gigantic building right in front of her. Two smooth, wide towers rose into the sky, each one tall enough to be a block of flats. Between them, two huge doors spanned the entrance. Massive figures were carved into the doors and along the sleek walls. They were illuminated at the bottom by flickering torches and they stretched up and away, their heads and shoulders disappearing into the night.

Gemma could see a small entrance at the bottom of one of the immense temple gates, like an opened door in an Advent calendar. The place seemed to buzz with activity, even though it was late evening. All sorts of people were milling around, passing in and out of the gigantic building. Boldly, Gemma walked right up to the gates and stepped through the tiny doorway, into the temple courtyard.

The courtyard seemed to be as wide as a football pitch. It was edged with massive marble pillars, and the silken surface of a high wall was just visible through the shadows. She hurried across the vast courtyard and slipped into the faintly glowing hall beyond.

There were less people here, but Gemma scurried onwards, over the polished stone floor. She passed through an archway into another apartment edged with pillars, where torches licked the walls, and lamps hung from the high ceiling.

This chamber was empty. Gemma hesitated. She could hear soft footsteps echoing in the distance. They grew louder and louder as they approached; Gemma slid behind one of the fat, white pillars.

A pretty young woman stepped into the chamber. Gemma recognised her instantly

51

– it was the woman from the procession! Now, in the torchlight, she could see a golden pendant around her neck. It was the same shape and size as Alexander's, with the falcon's head on it. This must be Alexander's double-crossing sister, Berenice.

The young woman looked about her, before stepping lightly across the marble floor and through a small doorway.

Gemma heard the deep, silky growl of a man's voice from the doorway as Berenice entered. Quietly, she crept after her, listening for a second and then, very cautiously, she poked her nose around the door.

Oil lamps stood all around the room. Glittering drapes cloaked the walls between burnished stone pillars, fluttering lightly over a gleaming floor. Very carefully, Gemma crept inside and slipped behind a curtain. The smooth, dark voice spoke again, and Gemma saw, standing at the far end of the room, the man she had seen earlier, riding in the procession behind Berenice. He stood straight and stock still. His immaculate white robe fell in smooth folds around him and his jewellery glinted in the flickering light.

"Well, have you found him yet?" he snapped.

Berenice approached him slowly and replied, "I've searched the whole city. He's nowhere to be found." Gemma could hear her voice tremble slightly.

"He must be somewhere," snarled the man.

"But Neos..." stuttered Berenice.

"Find him!" bellowed the man.

"Neos, it's a big city," she pleaded, her eyes wide with fear.

"You seem to forget that it might be the other way round." Neos spoke quietly this time, but there was no mistaking the menace in his voice. "If your brother had his way, it would be him here now, and you out there trembling and awaiting your death. You should thank me for the mercy I have shown you."

Berenice interrupted, "But I don't want – "

"Be quiet, you fool!" roared Neos. "You don't know what you want. You would be helpless without me. I have been your father's advisor for ten years, and I will be your advisor when you are ruler of Egypt.

But, if you are to be queen, we must first dispose of your brother!" Berenice fell silent and Neos clapped his hands sharply. A slave hurried in through the open door. Neos spoke to Berenice with a hiss.

"If your brother isn't already dead, then he soon will be. We will carry on with the plan as agreed." He addressed the slave who stood before him, his head bent low. "Bring the mourning cloaks – Alexander is dead." The slave looked up, shocked by the news. Then he quickly lowered his eyes and backed out of the room. Outside, Gemma could hear his grief-stricken cry and rushing footsteps as he ran to break the news to the rest of the household.

"My father will never believe it!" objected Berenice.

"You'd be surprised at some of the things your father believes," replied Neos scornfully.

"Well, I shall never believe a word you say!"

Neos dismissed her outburst with a flick of his hand. "Did you take the map from your brother's room?"

"That map was a gift to Alexander," objected Berenice.

"You forget, my dear, Alexander is dead. Now the map belongs to you. You will find it and bring it to me." Berenice stared at the floor.

"You were as keen to see that map as I was, once," Neos reminded her spitefully. "How you've changed, my dear. I used to think you had spirit!"

Berenice stood pale and trembling in the middle of the room. Neos turned away, rested his hand on an ice-cold pillar and began to drum his fingers until the slave returned with an armful of dark cloth. As he helped Neos and Berenice dress in their mourning clothes, Gemma slipped quietly out of the room.

She worked her way back to Soter's bakery, managing to correct a couple of wrong turns easily enough. Alexander was still asleep when she slipped back into the warm kitchen, but the soft thump of the door closing behind her woke him.

"What is it?" he asked sitting up and looking around.

"I'm over here," she said softly.

He saw her beside the door. "Have you been out?"

"Yes," she replied.

"Where?"

"I had to find out what was going on."

Gemma was relieved that she was not going to have to tell Alexander that his own sister had been conspiring against him. Neos was behind it – she knew that now. He had lied and bullied Berenice all the way. But she reasoned that it was still going to be a big shock for Alexander to discover that his father's trusted advisor was plotting against him.

"Hmmm," said Alexander thoughtfully, when she had told him everything.

"Hmmm?" exclaimed Gemma, stunned. "Aren't you shocked?"

"No – I've never liked him. I always thought there was something suspicious about him. You can see it in his eyes; he always looks as if he's doing a very hard sum in his head, like he's working something out, or planning something."

"He actually told Berenice that you

wanted to get rid of her," said Gemma.

"And she believed him?" asked Alexander, hurt creeping into his voice.

"She just looked scared to me. I think Neos must be threatening her."

"He threatened to drown my favourite hunting dog once."

"He did?"

"But father would never have allowed him to."

"So, he's frightened of your father?"

"My father is the Pharaoh. Even you'd be frightened of him!" Even you! Gemma smiled at the compliment.

"What was this map they were talking about?" she asked.

"I don't know," said Alexander, frowning and thinking hard.

"Do you have any maps?"

"Only a map of Egypt, drawn on papyrus. I can't think why Neos would want that." They fell silent for a moment, then Gemma spoke.

"It's still dark outside; I don't know what time it is, but I think we should try to sleep for a while. We're going to have a busy day tomorrow."

"Do you have a plan?" asked Alexander eagerly.

"Well, not a whole plan, but whatever happens, I expect we'll need all the rest we can get."

## 5. Trapped in the Mummy's Tomb

Gemma stood at the door of the bakery and swung her rucksack up over her shoulders. Alexander knelt and scratched a symbol of thanks into the earth floor.

"I shall reward Soter properly when we have sorted everything out, but for now he must think we are just two beggar children who are grateful for his kindness," said Alexander, with some of the old, princely grace that Gemma had seen yesterday. He stood up and, together, they slipped out of the bakery into the street.

Gemma had woken up before dawn. She had not been exactly sure what they should do, but she felt that, if Alexander could speak to Berenice, and convince her that Neos was the enemy of them both, then brother and sister might be able to face him together.

We must return to the temple and find her, she had decided, and it will be easier to get there in one piece while it's still dark. She had shaken Alexander gently, and together they had eaten the bread that Soter had left the night before.

Outside, the streets were dark and deserted, and the journey to the temple was even easier than Gemma had hoped. It wasn't long before the two children were crouched in a shop doorway opposite the massive front of the temple. The tiny door that had been open last night was this morning shut tight.

"Do you know any other way in?" asked Gemma.

"I'm afraid not," replied Alexander. "I have heard there is a secret passage that the priests use, but I don't know where it is."

"Perhaps the front door's not locked,"

suggested Gemma hopefully.

Suddenly, a loud noise came from behind the huge temple gates – a noise like a heavy table being scraped across a wooden floor. Light twinkled out from a tall crack between the doors and then flooded out as the gates were swung wide open. Gemma and Alexander ducked further back into the doorway.

"What's happening?" asked Gemma, as two camels sauntered out of the temple courtyard, followed by two more. They were being ridden by men, well wrapped up against the cool dawn air. More camels followed from behind, drawing wagons behind them. Slaves trotted on foot beside them, lighting the early morning gloom with flaming torches.

"Is it another procession?" asked Gemma.

"It looks as if someone's off on a trip. There are tents piled on to that wagon, and water barrels strapped on to that one over there. Look!" Alexander pointed.

"But why are they taking all those empty wagons with them?" asked Gemma, as six bare carts passed by in front of them. Then she noticed a tall man sitting high on the hump of a camel. "Isn't that Neos?" Gemma peered across the dim street. The torchlight illuminated the sharp features that poked out from beneath a dark hood.

Alexander nodded. "There's Berenice," he pointed. Gemma saw a smaller, dark figure, head bowed, perched on a camel beside him.

"Come on," said Gemma, "we must go with them. We have to try and speak to Berenice."

The two children crept forward, being careful to keep out of the torchlight. The front of the convoy was halfway along the street by now. Gemma and Alexander headed towards the last few trailing carts. There were no torchbearers this far back in the line, and the camel drivers were all concentrating hard on steering their animals along the city street. It was easy for Gemma and Alexander to creep up behind the last wagon and hurl themselves on the back as it rumbled slowly along.

They wriggled underneath an old rug that covered the collection of baskets and ropes, and peeked out at the buildings disappearing behind them.

Before long, the procession was out of the city altogether. Away from the buildings and people, the flat landscape glowed white in the moonlight and looked more like the snowy wastes of the North Pole than the desert. Above, the indigo sky was studded with sequin stars. On the horizon, a pale dawn crept upwards.

"I know this road," said Alexander. "It's the old way to Nefyria."

"Nefyria?" repeated Gemma. It was not a name that she had come across in any of her guidebooks.

"There are pyramids there. They were built by my forefathers, thousands of years ago," continued Alexander.

"Do they bury pharaohs there? Like in the pyramids at Giza?" asked Gemma.

"Not any more. Pyramids are much too easy to rob. Pharaohs are always buried with their treasure, so robbers break in and steal everything. My family are buried in secret caves now – no one but our priests know where. It's safer that way. But the people of Edfu believe that the pyramids of Nefyria have never been robbed."

"How come?"

"There are stories that Nefyria is protected by Anubis, the jackal god of the underworld. They say that robbers who enter the tombs will never come out again. They're too scared."

"So what's Neos doing coming out here?" asked Gemma.

The wagon rumbled onwards across the bare landscape, broken up only by a few prickly bushes and twisted trees. The sky was beginning to light up now, and a sliver of sun glowed on the horizon.

"It's going to be a long journey. The pyramids are a long way from the city. Hopefully, we'll be there before the sun is right up in the sky; it's going to get very hot under here," warned Alexander.

He was right. By the middle of the morning, Alexander and Gemma were sweltering beneath the heavy rug.

"I wish we had some water," Gemma

complained, and rolled slowly on to her back, crunching her rucksack beneath her. She lay still, flattened by the rug and the heat. "Do you still think we're going to Nefyria?"

"We've been heading south-east all morning – we're bound to reach the pyramids soon," said Alexander.

Suddenly, there was a shout in the distance, closely followed by the yelling and whooping of the other drivers – a message was being passed along the convoy. The wagon stopped. Gemma rolled back on to her stomach and peeped out from under the rug. She craned her neck to peer up ahead and saw that the whole wagon train had stopped. Drivers were leaping down and unharnessing their camels. Ahead, rising out of the flat, sandy landscape, Gemma could see the half-diamond shape of a stone pyramid. It was much bigger than she had expected. Parts of its smooth stone sides had crumbled away, revealing zigzagging steps underneath. Behind, in the distance she could see two other pyramids.

"Are we there?" asked Alexander, poking his head out beside her.

"Look out!" warned Gemma. The driver turned on his seat and dismounted as Gemma and Alexander ducked out of sight. He wandered up to the front of his wagon and began to unharness his camel. Gemma peered out once more.

"Quick, let's make a dash for that clump of bushes over there," she said, nudging Alexander with her hand. "Come on, while the driver's busy."

As quietly as they could, the two children slid out from underneath the rug and slipped on to the ground. Crouching and running at the same time, they scrambled over to the prickly bushes behind the wagon.

From their hiding place, they could see Neos in the distance. He was striding about, and they could hear him issuing orders. He seemed to be holding a small piece of parchment in his hand.

"Alexander, that must be the map Neos was talking about!" exclaimed Gemma. "Does it look familiar?"

Alexander squinted to get a better look. "It's hard to tell from here. It's not big enough to be my map of Egypt." He screwed up his eyes even tighter. "I can see a purple ribbon dangling from it. That looks familiar. I had a piece of papyrus in my treasure box tied with a purple ribbon."

"What was it?"

"I never thought of it as a map before. I always thought it was a drawing or a symbol or something. It was just a picture of a square with crosses and lines drawn on it."

"Where did you get it?"

"An old priest sent it to me before he died. He told me to treasure it. I didn't know what it was, so I put it in my treasure box. I haven't thought about it since."

"Well, Neos certainly has. You wait here, I'm going to take a closer look."

Gemma looked furtively around and scooted over to the wagon. The area was hectic with activity by now. People were erecting tents, wheeling wagons here and there, and unloading barrels of water. Chancing her luck, she wandered towards the pyramid, trying to appear as if she belonged to the wagon train. No one seemed to give her a second look as she passed.

Once she was closer, she lingered behind a heavy wooden cart and watched. Neos was holding the papyrus square close to his face and he was pacing slowly along the edge of the pyramid. He turned the parchment in his hand, and looked from the small piece of papyrus to the massive blocks of stone in front of him. Then he began to count, block by block, the number of stones from the corner of the pyramid. When he reached halfway, he looked back at the papyrus. Then he gave a shout, and began pointing to one particular block. Slaves immediately came running, armed with spades and ropes, and busied themselves digging and chipping away at the huge stone block.

The map is a plan of the tomb! thought Gemma – it must show the way in. What is Neos up to?

It took another half an hour before the slaves had scraped enough sand away to attach a rope around the block and begin heaving it out of place. Even then, it was a long, hard job to dislodge it. As they worked, Neos paced around them, trying to see into the gaps and cursing impatiently under his breath. Gemma stood still and watched until, with a final shout of triumph, the slaves managed to pull the stone far enough out of the side of the pyramid for a man to squeeze through.

"Torch! Bring me a torch!" shouted Neos, waving his hand in the air. Instantly, a torch was lit and brought over to him. He snatched it, pushed a slave out of the way and squeezed into the dark gap.

A moment later, he squeezed out again.

"That's it!" he cried. "The way in." He waved over to Berenice who had been sitting on a piece of rock. A slave was shielding her from the sun with a large palm fan and another was trying to persuade her to take a cushion to sit on, but Berenice just sat, watching Neos. When she saw him waving to her, she looked away.

"Move this stone out of the way!"

shouted Neos. "Bring torches and sacks! Hurry!"

Before long, the secret entrance to the pyramid was clear and Neos stood at the head of a gang of slaves, all carrying torches and holding sacks.

"Sosibus!" he said, pointing to a tall, solemn-looking slave at the head of the gang. "You go in first!" Sosibus hesitated. The other slaves looked towards him nervously. Sosibus spoke.

"What about the curse? What about Anubis?"

"In!" roared Neos. Sosibus did not argue. He turned and bravely entered the small opening in the pyramid. Neos followed, and four more slaves crept in after him.

Once they were all out of sight, Gemma stepped forward. The other members of the party were busy setting up camp. Berenice was still sitting on her rock, staring at the ground.

Gemma tiptoed to the edge of the pyramid and peered into the gap. Two spare torches had been left burning near the entrance. She picked one up. In front of her, a low, square tunnel stretched away into blackness. Neos and his slaves had disappeared into the gloom. Gemma crept in after them, stooping as she edged her way forward. The floor was hard beneath a thin covering of sand. It sloped downwards and straight ahead.

Before long, Gemma saw a faint glow in front of her. As she approached, she realised that it was the entrance to a chamber deep inside the pyramid. A heavy stone door stood open. She carefully laid her torch, still burning, on the sandy floor and crept towards the light. She could hear Neos giving orders to his men who were shuffling around inside. She flattened herself against the tunnel wall and looked in; there was Neos. Around him, in the dancing light, Gemma could see all the treasures of the long-dead Pharaoh. Golden goblets, silver plates, jewellery, neatly rolled rugs – it looked like an Aladdin's cave, and Gemma felt her heart flutter with anticipation.

Beside the doorway there was a stone column. Silently, she sneaked into the chamber and hid herself behind it.

The slaves were busy, stuffing everything they could lay their hands on into sacks. Neos wove his way around them, picking up treasures here and there to examine them more closely. His eyes sparkled greedily as his men steadily stripped the cave of its riches.

At that moment, Gemma felt something small push against her boot. She moved her foot a little and heard a hiss. Something slithered around her ankle. With a cry she leaped backwards, shaking her leg fiercely until the slithering sensation stopped. Her cry echoed around the walls. Peeking out, Gemma could see Neos and his men staring straight at her. She froze.

"Well, well!" purred Neos. "Is this a ghost? Are you a spirit, protecting your dead Pharaoh? A servant of Anubis, perhaps?" He strode towards her, a thin smile curling his lips. "You don't look very much like a spirit to me." He was standing beside her now. "You look more like an inquisitive child." He bent down towards her, and she stared straight into his cold, hard eyes.

"Who are you?" he asked nastily. Gemma tried to steady her breath.

"Gemma..." she said.

"What are you doing in my tomb?"

"I – I wanted to see what a mummy looks like," replied Gemma boldly.

"Well, I suppose that can be arranged," said Neos, and straightened up. He turned to Sosibus. "Get everyone out of here! Take everything you can carry and leave – now!" Hastily, Sosibus began to give orders to the other slaves, who started gathering up what remained of the treasure. Then he herded them out through the open doorway.

Once they had all gone, Neos turned back to Gemma.

"Well," he said, "now's your chance to see a real mummy – in the flesh, or what used to be flesh!" He laughed menacingly. Gemma looked up at him.

"Go on!" He pointed towards the large stone sarcophagus that lay in the middle of the room. The ransacking slaves had managed to heave the lid off, and clouds of sandy dust still hung in the air. She edged her way nervously towards the sarcophagus. She could hear Neos move behind her. Turning around, she saw him gather up the two remaining torches and stride towards the door. He stood in the doorway and laughed.

"Take a good look, because it's going to be the last thing you'll ever see!" Then he swept out of the chamber, his evil laughter echoing eerily about the walls.

Gemma heard a heavy scraping noise as the wide stone door was slowly eased back into place. Then she saw nothing. As the door closed, the last ray of light from the torches disappeared, and Gemma was left alone in the darkness.

## 6. The Curse of Anubis

Until now, Gemma hadn't noticed how cold it was. The tomb had never seen sunlight, and the warmth outside could not pierce the thick stone walls of the pyramid. She shivered, half from cold, half from fright. She was trapped! She thought of edging through the darkness to the door – perhaps she could push it open? But then, with a shudder, she remembered the snake that had slithered across her foot. Where was the snake now? Gemma didn't dare move.

Trying to think rationally, she remembered her rucksack. She'd forgotten all about it, slung on her back. Without moving her feet, she bent her arm out of one of its straps and swung it down in front of her. Holding it safely off the floor, she rummaged through the clothes and the bundle of Alexander's jewellery, down to the sweet wrappers still littering the bottom.

There! She'd found it! Her tiny pen torch felt slim and smooth between her fingers. She pulled it out and flicked it on, waving the tiny beam of light on the floor around her feet, checking for snakes. The ground was clear. Gemma spun around. Neos and his men had done a good job ransacking the cave. She hurried across the tomb and checked the door. Thin streams of air were seeping in around its edges. She pushed; the great weight of it budged slightly, but no more. It felt as though a latch on the other side was holding it shut. Perhaps she could find something to thread through the gap at the edge of the door, something thin enough to pass all the way through, yet strong enough to lift up the catch.

Perhaps there was a knife or a sword buried with the mummy? She had read about the Egyptians burying their dead with their most treasured possessions. She knew she had no choice – Gemma approached the sarcophagus and peered over the cold, stone rim. She stared in awe at the beautifully decorated mummy case that lay inside. It was the one thing in the room that Neos had not tampered with. Perhaps he was frightened of Anubis after all; or maybe she had distracted him.

Holding her torch close, she shone its light down the length of the case. The likeness of a pharaoh was painted on the top. It had thick, stripy hair which framed a smooth, brown face and the two arms were folded neatly on top of the body. Someone had spent long, loving hours decorating this inner coffin – Gemma was moved.

Taking a deep breath, she pushed the beautifully painted lid to one side. It moved very slowly. She pushed again. The lid slid open far enough for Gemma to see the crumbling bandaged head of the mummified pharaoh within. The bandages were brown, and a delicate smell of chemicals and herb tea wafted out. The mummy seemed tiny! This Pharaoh couldn't have been much bigger than me – even before they shrink-wrapped him, thought Gemma.

She shone her torch inside the mummy's case, searching for a knife. Suddenly, something beside the mummy glinted in the beam of light. Cautiously, she reached inside and touched the sharp edges of what felt like a metal lump. She groped around – it seemed to be a small statue. Gemma carefully closed her fingers around the cold shape and pulled.

As the mysterious object emerged from under the lid, she held it directly under the bright torchlight. It was the statue of a cat, ears pricked, head held proudly, golden and encrusted with green jewels! She remembered the tiny statuette that she had exchanged for her beggar's clothes; it was a life-size version of that. The Pharaoh must have treasured it. Out of all his riches, he had chosen this to be buried beside him. Gemma pushed it back under the lid, not wanting to disturb the mummy any further.

She looked around the chamber, picking out the unfamiliar shapes with her torch.

A few stone plinths stood around the edge of the tomb. One at a time, she searched them, moving aside plain metal pots, clay bead necklaces and dull paste brooches. There was no sign of anything that might help her open the latch. With a sigh, she tried the last plinth.

Sticking out from beneath a large, earthenware plate, Gemma's torchlight picked out a handle. It was smooth and wooden, and exactly the sort of shape that might fit into the palm of a hand, like a knife handle! She touched it, but it seemed to be stuck firmly beneath the plate. She took hold of it and pulled.

A loud clanking noise made her jump. Spinning her torch around, Gemma looked to see a small square of stone disappear into the wall behind her, leaving a dark gap in the smooth rock surface. The handle twitched beneath her fingers. A secret opening, thought Gemma, as her heart leaped – the handle must have been the trigger to unlock it!

Wasting no time, she rushed over to the opening and peered inside. Her torchlight stretched away into the darkness. A tunnel! Gemma rushed back to collect her rucksack before squeezing herself through the small, square opening. This is an escape route just big enough for a dead Pharaoh who was afraid of the dark, she thought, as she wriggled her way forwards. The tunnel sloped upwards. Gemma's progress was slow, but she didn't care as long as she was travelling towards the surface and daylight.

At the end of the tunnel there appeared to be a dead end – there was something blocking her way out. She reached forwards and ran her fingers over the rock, following her hand with her torch. Just as she had hoped, there was a perfectly circular hole chipped out of the stone. Checking inside with her torch first, she placed her finger in the hole, hooking it into a small gap inside and squeezing at the stone like a trigger. There was a click. The tiny passage door moved a little, and then a lot as Gemma pushed it wide.

Warm air flooded in and bathed her. It felt wonderful! Without hesitating, she squirmed her way out of the hole and stood up. She must have come out behind the pyramid. She hurried to a corner and looked around the edge – no one there. I hope they haven't left already, thought Gemma, alarmed for a second. Then she heard the sound of voices. She rushed towards the last corner and lay down on her stomach to peek around the edge. There was Neos, amid large sacks full of treasure. He was crouched, rummaging and gloating over his spoils. Sosibus and the other slaves had all moved away from the pyramid. They whispered to one another, keeping an eye on the passageway as if they expected Anubis himself, jackal jaws slavering and sharp teeth glinting in the sunlight, to rush out and drag Neos inside.

Suddenly, Neos looked up.

"Where is it?" he bellowed. "Where's the emerald cat?" The slaves stood still and Sosibus shook his head.

"Why isn't it here? You fools have left it in the tomb! You idiots!"

Furiously, Neos stood up and strode back towards the tomb. He grabbed a torch that was still burning in the entrance, and disappeared inside.

The servants scuttled further away from the pyramid and busied themselves, frightened that Neos would reappear and order them to return with him into the tomb.

When she was sure that no one was looking, Gemma crept out from her hiding place and sneaked to the open door of the passageway. She darted inside, flicking her torch on once more, following Neos back down the secret path to the Pharaoh's tomb.

Inside the chamber, she could hear the scraping of the mummy case's lid, as Neos pushed it back further to search the mummy's body for the precious emerald cat. Gemma eased herself between the passage wall and the open door of the chamber. She had to delay Neos, and give Alexander a chance to speak with Berenice. If Neos were trapped inside, it would be a while before the slaves dared to come back down and look for him. Heaving with all her might, Gemma began to push the door closed. She heard Neos shout, alerted by the scraping of the door on the sandy floor. She pushed as hard as she could; his footsteps were padding quickly towards the doorway. She gave one last, desperate shove. Thunk! The stone door shut heavily and the latch flipped back into place. Gemma heard Neos hammering on the other side. That should hold him for a while, she thought, and turned to leave. Now, she must find Alexander.

At that moment, a terrible scream echoed from inside the tomb. Gemma froze, terrified by the bloodcurdling noise. The scream came again, and this time it continued...on and on, horribly. Gemma ducked back into the shadows and switched off her torch. There was a shallow niche in the wall, and she pressed herself into it just in time.

Rushing down the passageway came the slaves, Sosibus first, armed with fiery torches. Their wide eyes shone in the flickering light. Sosibus unlatched the door hurriedly and tugged it open.

Inside the tomb, a sputtering torch lay on the ground. The slaves edged slowly into the chamber. Neos was lying face down on the ground. Sosibus was the only one to approach him, and he did so gingerly. Crouching down, he rolled Neos gently on to his back. His eyes were staring wide open. The scream was frozen on his open lips, and his face was contorted with fear. In his hands, gripped between white fingers, was the emerald cat statue.

The other slaves backed away in fright when they saw him. But Sosibus stayed where he was and whispered "Anubis!"

Another slave repeated the word, his voice fearful with respect. Then the others began to mutter to themselves.

"Anubis, Anubis," they murmured, slowly retreating from the tomb. None of them spotted Gemma as they passed her, backing away up the tunnel.

Only Sosibus remained. Gemma stayed motionless as she watched him squatting beside the body. Gently, he prised the emerald cat from Neos' frozen fingers. Holding it as though it had just come from a hot oven, he carried it over to the sarcophagus and laid it carefully beside the mummy. He whispered a prayer under his breath and bowed, long and low, touching his forehead as he did so. Then he returned to Neos. He laid his torch on the ground, bent down and picked the body up in his arms. He turned and slowly carried it out of the chamber, past Gemma and up the passageway into the daylight.

Trembling, Gemma slipped out of her hiding place. She fought the urge to run after Sosibus and out of the shadows – her curiosity was too much for her. Tentatively, she crept into the tomb. What had killed Neos? Surely the story of the mummy's curse couldn't be true! In the light of Sosibus' torch, Gemma scanned the room for clues. Everything was exactly as she had left it, except for the gaping lid of the mummy case and the long dent in the sand where Neos had fallen.

Then she heard a familiar hiss. Startled, she looked around the floor. There, slipping away into the shadows, was a small, brown, deadly snake.

Gemma turned and ran.

## 7. Neos' Final Journey

Outside, Sosibus carried Neos' body to a gnarled tree and laid him in the shade of the thorny branches. Slaves stood around, silent now. Berenice knelt beside the body and tentatively touched its hand. No one saw Gemma slip out of the pyramid and hurry past the wagons to the spot where she had left Alexander.

By the time she reached him, he was bursting with excitement.

"You've been gone for ages," he said, as soon as Gemma came within hearing distance. "What's going on? What's all the fuss about?"

"You won't believe what's happened!"

said Gemma.

"What? What?" he urged her, and she told him everything.

"Now it's up to you," she finished. "You have to speak to Berenice." Alexander nodded gravely. "I suppose there's no time like the present," he said.

He stepped out from behind the clump of bushes and walked past the wagons and camels, towards the gathering beneath the tree. Pushing his way gently through the crowd of slaves, he stood behind his sister.

"Berenice," he began in a calm, dignified voice. He didn't know how she would react to seeing him again, but the doubt in his mind and his heart did not show itself in his voice. Berenice spun around where she knelt. "Alexander!" she exclaimed. She leaped to her feet and embraced her brother. "Oh, Alexander! I was really beginning to think that you were dead!" She squeezed him harder and Alexander hugged her back for a moment, before drawing away.

They looked at each other, then Berenice spoke.

"Forgive me for failing to stop Neos."

"He is a hard man to thwart," said Alexander, giving a small smile.

"He *was* a hard man to thwart," Berenice corrected him. They smiled at each other happily.

Late the next morning, Gemma stood beside Alexander in the bazaar, back at Edfu. At Nefyria, they had helped Berenice and the slaves to carry all the Pharaoh's treasures back into his tomb, and buried Neos beside the place where he had committed his final crime. Then large, colourful tents had been erected around an enormous, crackling fire and Gemma, Alexander and Berenice had stretched out on silky-soft rugs while slaves bustled to and fro with large plates of spicy, sweet food. They had slept beneath the wide, starry sky and travelled back to the city at first light.

"Won't you come and meet my father?" asked Alexander, looking over the shabby stalls to the temple beyond. "He will want to thank you for helping me."

"No, I really can't. I must return to my family," said Gemma ruefully. Then she remembered the bundle of Alexander's jewels still tucked away in her rucksack, and fumbled through her bag before handing them back to him.

He shook his head. "Keep them," he insisted.

"I couldn't," said Gemma firmly. "They're yours."

"But I must give you something, so that you remember me," objected Alexander. "Wait here," he said, and disappeared into the crowd.

When he returned a few minutes later, he was grinning and carrying something curled up in the palm of his hand.

"Here!" He opened his fingers and dropped a small golden object into Gemma's hand. It was the little jewelled cat. Gemma gasped.

"But where did you find it?" she exclaimed.

"On a stall – those beggars must have sold it. Now it is yours again."

Gemma smiled. "Thank you, Alexander," she said warmly, and she leaned forward and kissed him lightly on the cheek. Then she turned and pushed her way into the crowd.

It didn't take her long to find a quiet back street. As she unfastened the necklace, she wondered whether to change back into her normal clothes, but by then it was too late. The world seemed to spin around, faster and faster. With a jolt, Gemma found herself standing in front of Mum and Magda again. Quickly, she jammed the necklace into her rucksack.

"Where did you get that outfit?" was the first thing they said when they saw her. Gemma's mother pursed her lips thoughtfully. "Hmm, that looks very authentic, but I think it might be a bit too scruffy to wear back home. Come on, Gemma, we've been wondering where you had disappeared to – come and see the stalls we've been looking at!"

Dad was at the airport to pick them up when they arrived back in England.

"Glad to be back?" he asked Gemma, once they had loaded their luggage into the boot and squeezed into the car.

Gemma sighed uncertainly. "Hmmm."

"I don't think she wanted to come

home," said Mum. "She's been acting like Cleopatra ever since Edfu!"

"Did you meet any pharaohs while you were there?" joked Dad.

"I met a pharaoh's son," said Gemma, in a regal voice.

"See what I mean!" laughed Mum.

When they reached home, Gemma went straight to her bedroom. She heaved her suitcase on to her bed and opened it. Tucked at the bottom was the beggar's outfit, and underneath it was the little jewelled cat, lying on top of the purple and green beaded necklace. Carefully, she laid out the tattered tunic on the bed, then lifted the necklace and the jewelled cat out of the case. She stood the glittering cat on the table beside her bed. Then she knelt on the floor and pulled the small wooden jewellery box from under her bed. Delicately, she placed the purple and green necklace inside and closed the lid.

"Goodbye Alexander," she whispered, "and good luck."

The piles of books about Egypt were still sitting on the floor. Gemma reached over and dragged one pile nearer. The red, shiny paperback lay on top. Picking it up, she flicked through it once more. There was the chapter on Edfu, and the page about Alexander. She scanned the words, then she scanned them again. To her delight and surprise, the paragraph which had described Alexander's mysterious disappearance had completely vanished.

For the first time since she had arrived home, Gemma smiled.